CONTENTS

Jamie Morgan sprinted along the beach of Ammonite Bay to meet his new best friend.

"Have you got everything?" asked Tess Clay, jumping off the rock she was standing on. "I brought my binoculars and my compass."

Jamie took off his backpack and rummaged inside for his fossil hunting

DINOSAUR CLUB

A Triceratops Charge

Written by Rex Stone
Illustrated by Louise Forshaw

Jamie has just moved to Ammonite Bay, a
stretch of coastline famed for its fossils. Jamie is
a member of Dinosaur Club – a network of
kids who share dinosaur knowledge, help identify
fossils, post new discoveries, and chat about
all things prehistoric. Jamie carries his tablet
everywhere in case he needs to contact the Club.

Jamie is exploring Ammonite Bay when he
meets Tess, another member of Dinosaur Club.
Tess takes Jamie to a cave with a strange tunnel
and some dinosaur footprints. When they walk
along the footprints, the two new friends find
themselves back in the time of the dinosaurs!

It's amazing, but dangerous too – and they'll
definitely need help from the Dinosaur Club…

equipment. "I've got my pocket knife and my notebook. Oh, and my tablet, of course!" Jamie never went anywhere without his tablet, in case he needed to contact the Dinosaur Club – a network of kids around the world who loved everything prehistoric. "I brought some sandwiches, too," Jamie said. "Cheese and Granddad's homemade chilli chutney. It'll blow your head off!"

"I can't wait to get back to our cave," Tess said.

"You mean you can't wait to get back to the dinosaurs!" Jamie said, as the two friends hurried down the beach. Jamie had met Tess for the first time yesterday and together they had discovered Ammonite Bay's biggest secret: an amazing world of living dinosaurs! First, Jamie had found a set of fossilized dinosaur footprints, and then the footprints had transported them to a place where dinosaurs still lived.

"It's hard keeping something so big a secret," Tess confessed. "My brother kept asking me what I did yesterday."

"I know!" Jamie replied. "My mum got a huge Triceratops skull fossil for the museum this morning, and I kept thinking about the real Triceratops we saw yesterday."

Jamie and his mum had moved in with his granddad to the old lighthouse on the cliffs. Jamie's mum was a palaeontologist, and she planned to open a dinosaur museum on the ground floor.

She knew more about dinosaurs than anyone, but she didn't know the colours of a T. rex like Jamie and Tess did!

"Luckily we can tell Dinosaur Club all about Dino World," said Tess.

"I wasn't sure they'd believe us," Jamie said. "I'm really glad they did!"

Jamie's tablet had been buzzing all evening with excited messages from their Dinosaur Club friends. In fact, Dino World was now an official club secret. "I forgot to tell you!" panted Jamie, as they scrambled up the steep path towards their secret cave. "I brought some pencils with me. I thought we could make a map of Dino World in my notebook."

"Good idea," Tess said.

"We'll be like real explorers, charting unknown territories!"

"And seeing lots of dinosaurs!"

They reached the tall stack of boulders that led to their secret cave, and climbed up using cracks in the rock. From the top of the boulders, Jamie could see his granddad's coastguard boat patrolling the bay.

Jamie quickly slipped into the dark cave, but Tess paused at the hidden entrance. "What if Dino World's not there?" she asked. "What if we dreamt it?"

Jamie laughed, and the sound echoed around the cave. "No way! That T. rex we met was definitely real!" With a shiver of excitement, he turned on his torch and shone it into the far corner. The beam picked out the small gap in the cave wall.

Jamie took off his backpack and crawled into the second chamber, which was narrower and pitch dark. Jamie and Tess suspected they were the only people ever to have been in this place.

Jamie flashed his torch over the stone floor. "Here are the fossilized dinosaur footprints we found yesterday."

"The best fossil anyone has ever found!" Tess said. The footprints had somehow transported them to Dino World.

Tess stepped over the first clover-shaped indent in the cave floor. "Here goes!" She placed her foot carefully over each footprint, walking in the dinosaur tracks.

Jamie stuck close behind her and counted every step. "One... two... three... four... FIVE!"

In an instant, the cold, damp cave was gone and Jamie and Tess were standing in a bright, sunny cave and staring out at giant, sun-dappled trees. The air was hot and humid, and they could hear the heavy drone of insects. They ran out on to the damp ground of Dino World.

"We're back in the jungle," said Jamie happily. "We're on Ginkgo Hill."

"This is so cool!" said Tess, looking eagerly around.

Jamie laughed. "Boiling, you mean!" He picked up a large leaf off the ground and fanned himself. Suddenly he stopped. "What was that?"

The two friends listened hard. From somewhere in the steaming jungle they could hear scuffling – and it was getting nearer.

"Something's coming!" warned Tess.

Just then, a plump, scaly little creature with a flat, bony head burst out from a clump of ferns. It scuttled along on its hind legs and hurled itself at Jamie, knocking him flat on his back.

Grunk! Grunk! Grunk!

"It's Wanna!" exclaimed Tess in relief.

Jamie and Tess had met the little dinosaur on their first visit to Dino World, and the Dinosaur Club had told them he was a Wannanosaurus. Wanna had helped them escape from the T. rex and had turned out to be a true friend.

"Stop rubbing me, Wanna!" panted Jamie, trying to push him off. "Your head's rougher than sandpaper."

Tess reached up to the ginkgo tree and picked a handful of the small, foul-smelling fruit. She held one out. "Have a stink-o bomb, Wanna. Your favourite!"

Wanna bounded over and greedily gobbled it up as Jamie staggered to his feet. Tess gave him one more and then quickly tossed a few more pieces of the fruit to Jamie, who hid them in his backpack.

"Let's start mapping!" said Tess.

Wanna sniffed the bag as Jamie dug around and pulled out his notebook and pencils. "We're here," he said, drawing Ginkgo Hill in the middle of the page. He put the four points of the compass in the corner of the map.

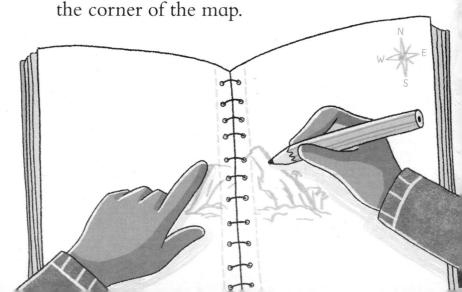

"Yesterday we found the ocean and the lagoon in the west." He sketched them in.

Tess checked the compass. "So let's head north today."

"Great," said Jamie. "Come on, Wanna! We're going exploring."

Wanna wagged his tail and trotted happily alongside them. They scrambled through ferns and squelched among slimy toadstools.

At last they came to a break in the trees and peered through. Below was the dense tangle of the jungle and beyond that a vast green plain with a wide river snaking through towards their hill.

"Look at those far away mountains," said Tess. "They're so high their peaks are hidden in the clouds."

Jamie scanned the horizon with the binoculars. "Far Away Mountains – that's a good name!" He scribbled it down on the map.

Then Jamie scanned the plain, and what he saw nearly made him drop his binoculars. There were about fifteen strange-looking houses made of orange earth sitting near a curve in the river.

"What is it?" Tess asked.

"I don't know," Jamie replied. "I think... I think there's a village of houses!"

CHAPTER 2

"No way!" Tess said. She grabbed the binoculars and gasped. "I thought we were the only people in Dino World."

"Me too," said Jamie. "But… who could they be? There weren't any people around during dinosaur times. Humans didn't come along for millions of years!"

"Well, if *we're* here," Tess reasoned,

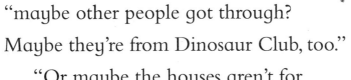

"maybe other people got through? Maybe they're from Dinosaur Club, too."

"Or maybe the houses aren't for people at all, but something else," Jamie guessed, as he added this odd discovery to his map. "How should I label it?"

"I'm not sure," Tess admitted. "Since we don't know what they are, we need to investigate. That's what real explorers would do!"

Following Tess's compass, the two friends set off north-east down the rest of Ginkgo Hill. Wanna made excited grunks as he clambered over roots and ferns. The trunks of giant trees rose into the misty canopy and insects as big and colourful as parrots buzzed around their heads.

Soon they heard splashing water and found themselves on the banks of a wide river that cut the forest in two.

"We'll have to swim for it if we're going to get to those houses." Tess said as she started down the bank.

"Wait!" warned Jamie, peeling off his backpack and pulling out his tablet. He opened the Dinosaur Club app, tapped the DinoData section, and typed in *'prehistoric river creatures'*.

"We might meet one of these," he said, handing the tablet to Tess.

"Champsosaurus," read Tess. "Hmm. Looks like a crocodile."

"And we'd look like its dinner!"

Jamie peered into the water for signs of life and spotted several greyish humps. "Look over there."

"Those are stones, fossil-brain," Tess said. "We can cross there!"

When the three of them reached
the other side, Tess checked her compass
again and they headed off through
the trees.

"How long do you think it'll take us
to get to the houses?" Tess asked.

"Hard to tell," puffed Jamie. "But
we've got to figure out what those things
are for our map."

They stumbled into a large clearing
surrounded by three walls of creepers.
Spiky plants grew all over the ground,
and Wanna grabbed a clump in his
mouth and chomped happily.

"Okay, Wanna. Lunchtime!" declared
Jamie. He climbed onto a log and tore
the foil off the cheese and spicy chilli
chutney sandwiches. He was just handing
a sandwich to Tess when Wanna leapt up
and grabbed half of it in his mouth.

"Hey, that's my lunch!" exclaimed Tess. Wanna chewed greedily. Suddenly, the little dinosaur blinked in surprise and began to run around in circles, shaking his head and making strange gak-gak noises.

"He's discovered Granddad's spicy
chilli chutney!" Jamie laughed.

A deep rumbling sound from the
forest made Jamie and Tess instantly
stop laughing.

"Only something really big could
make that noise," murmured Tess,
glancing over her shoulder. "What
if it's the T. rex again?"

"Wait – I can hear mooing," said Jamie, puzzled. His attention was fixed on the wall of creepers nearest to them.

"Like a herd of giant cows," said Tess.

There was a sound of snapping and splitting vines. Jamie and Tess leapt to their feet as the creepers just in front of them began to shake. Jamie dropped his sandwich as the last strands tore away.

A massive beaked head with three huge horns peered into the clearing.

CHAPTER 3

"It's a Triceratops!" whispered Jamie, staring at the giant head looming above him. "Awesome!"

Jamie and Tess could feel its hot breath on their faces. With a snort, the dinosaur forced its body through the creepers and took a lumbering step into the clearing.

"I'm glad it's not a T. rex," Tess said. "But I can't believe it's so gigantic!"

"Mum was telling me about Triceratops this morning," said Jamie. "It weighs more than an elephant!"

"I don't want that treading on my toes!" Tess hastily scrambled onto the log and pulled Jamie up behind her.

The creepers shook again and another Triceratops pushed its way into the clearing. Soon a whole herd of the three-horned creatures stomped into view.

One Triceratops put his head down to eat some of the ferns right in front of them. The herd munched on the plants, completely ignoring the two friends.

"Look, Wanna!" Jamie said, as the little dinosaur gobbled up a flower nearby. "They're herbivores, like you, which means they won't want to eat us."

"That's true, but if one steps on us, it would be just as dangerous!" replied Tess. "We better not risk trying to walk through them. Maybe we should try to scare them away from the clearing?"

"I don't think scaring a herd of Triceratops would be a good idea," Jamie said. "They might end up charging like a herd of elephants!"

They heard a moo from the biggest dinosaur in the herd. The sound rumbled around the clearing as the others took up the call. It shook Jamie and Tess on their log.

"The leader's given a signal," Tess said. "What does it mean?"

"I think it means they're moving on!" said Jamie. "And they're going in the direction of the houses."

They both tried to keep their balance as their log was bumped from all sides by the tree trunk-sized legs going by, but it was too much! Jamie slipped off the log and had to roll away quickly to avoid being trampled.

"What are we going to do?" Jamie said, breathlessly, as he scrambled safely back onto the log. "We've got to get away from their feet!"

"It seems to me that the safest place is on top of a Triceratops!" Tess said. "Otherwise, we'll be squished!"

"Fossil-brain!" squeaked Jamie. "We would need a trampoline to get up there."

"Maybe we don't," Tess said. "Look, that Triceratops is smaller than the others. I think it must be a young one."

She pulled some ginkgoes out of Jamie's bag and held one out. The younger beast stopped and sniffed the air. Then it turned its head to face the pair of them, and gave a blasting snort

that nearly blew Jamie and Tess off the log. Tess quickly dropped the ginkgo onto the ground and the beast lowered its big head, and its frill was in their reach. Its powerful jaws ground noisily as it chewed the orange fruit.

Tess tossed several other ginkgoes onto the ground and whispered, "Now, we can try to climb on board."

Tess quickly took hold of the frill and pulled herself onto the Triceratops's forehead, being careful not to frighten it. Then she reached down and gave Jamie a hand up. Soon they were each sitting

on the leathery neck and holding on to one of the Triceratops's horns.

"We're away from the huge legs, but what if it throws us off?" Jamie asked.

"I don't think it even realises we're here!" Tess replied.

Their Triceratops finished its ginkgoes and then it raised its head and began to follow the herd. Wanna stared up at them, his head on one side.

"Hey, Wanna," waved Tess. "Look at us!"

"This is awesome!" declared Jamie. "It's like being on the handlebars of a giant bike!"

"Hold tight for a bumpy ride!" said Tess.

The dinosaur swayed as it walked steadily through the tangle of jungle creepers and trees. Jamie and Tess slid about, dodging the passing branches while Wanna trotted among the legs of the herd, grunking at the top of his voice.

"This is much faster than walking!" laughed Jamie.

Suddenly they could see bright light through the giant leaves and branches. The herd left the jungle behind and lumbered out into the dazzling sunlight of the plain.

CHAPTER 4

Jamie squinted at the open land shimmering in the heat.

"Look!" He pointed. "There's the river again – it comes down from the mountains." He leaned his notebook on the Triceratops's horn and drew a winding line from the mountain peaks across the plain to the jungle.

"In a way, we're the first people ever to make a map!" said Tess as the herd moved steadily across the sweltering plain.

"The first explorers, riding out on safari," declared Jamie, laughing. "This is great. I can see for miles!"

"Look at all these fantastic dinosaurs," Tess said. She pointed to a slow-moving herd grazing on the leaves of some trees and spoke to an imaginary camera. "This is Tess Clay, reporting live from Dino World, on the Great Plain. Who needs a jeep when you have the luxury of T-Tops Travel?"

Jamie laughed. He knew Tess wanted to be a famous wildlife presenter on TV one day.

Tess went on. "Here we are watching the Alamosauruses reaching their long necks to the highest branches, and further in the distance we can see the strange dwellings that we are about to investigate. Stay tuned for what could be the most exciting discovery of all time!"

The Triceratops lumbered on as they watched the scenery go by.

"Can you see that weird rock there?" said Tess, checking her compass. "Over to the east."

"It looks like a huge fang," Jamie said.
"Let's call it Fang Rock!" He drew in the
pointy rock and labelled it. Then he
looked up. "Hey, we're really close to the
houses now." He put his notebook away.
"They're at least three times as tall
as my dad!"

The thin towers stood in a silent
group in the baking heat, silent and
seemingly empty.

"I don't think they are houses," said
Jamie. The mounds were made out of
bumpy orange dirt and had deep crevices
running down them. There weren't any
windows or doors, and Jamie couldn't
imagine what kind of creature could
live in it.

"There's no sign of any dinosaurs," said Tess. "This feels weird."

"As if something's waiting to happen." Jamie whispered.

The herd stopped a little way from the strange towers and mooed.

"They're signalling again," said Tess. "They don't seem to like the towers either."

"Let's see if anyone in Dinosaur Club knows what they are," said Jamie, taking out his tablet. He took a photo of the towers.

"Back in the Cretaceous!" he typed.

"Anyone know what these are?"

In came a rush of messages.

"Cool! Rock formations?" suggested Eva from Mexico.

Adi from Indonesia wrote, "Looks like giant insect nests."

Meanwhile, the Triceratops were still mooing anxiously at the strange towers.

"I don't think Wanna understands their language," Tess said.

Instead of being cautious, Wanna was scrabbling excitedly at the bottom of one of the towers.

"They're termite nests," wrote Natasha from Russia. "Make sure you don't disturb them ..."

All of a sudden, a stream of orange, ant-like insects was pouring out of the hole and all over Wanna. The little dinosaur jumped back, batting at his face with his claws.

"Woah!" gasped Tess. "There are so many of them!"

The termites kept streaming from the towers. Jamie had never seen anything like it. Wanna was yelping and shaking himself as they crawled all over him.

"Luckily Wanna is too quick for them," said Jamie, as the little dinosaur did a frantic dance.

"He's flinging them off with all that jerking around!"

"But he's scaring the Triceratops!" Tess cried.

The Triceratops stamped their feet in alarm and backed off, jostling each other. The shaking seemed to wake more of the termites up. Now thousands of them were pouring out of every mound. Jamie saw the insects stream up the legs of the leader of the herd and into its eyes and nose.

The leader tossed its head like an angry bull to shake the insects off but it was no use. It couldn't move as easily as small, agile Wanna. Suddenly it bellowed in terror and charged straight through the termite city! Dry dirt and insects scattered everywhere.

Jamie and Tess felt their Triceratops lurching forward, as the other dinosaurs began to run.

"It's a stampede!" yelled Jamie, stuffing his tablet into his backpack.

"Hold on!"

They clung to the horns as the herd took off through the cloud of orange dust. Jamie felt like a rodeo rider being bucked about. Then he felt a prickle on his leg and looked down to see a termite crawling on him. Despite the bumping, Jamie managed to flick it away quickly. But soon, a whole army of termites was crawling over their Triceratops's head towards him.

Jamie tried to knock away the ones that crawled onto him, but all of the movement made his backpack slip from his shoulder! He flung out an arm to catch it as it fell, but it was too late.

Jamie's backpack tumbled to the ground and disappeared beneath the cloud of dust.

Jamie couldn't believe it.

He had lost his precious tablet and his notebook and there was nothing he could do about it.

Insects were scuttling all over him now, crawling in his hair and down his neck.

"Yuck!" Jamie wailed as one termite crawled across his face. He managed to flick it away.

"This is horrible!" cried Tess, shaking termites off her arms and legs.

They tried to ignore the insects crawling over them and just clung on for dear life.

"Where's Wanna?" yelled Tess.

"I don't know," Jamie shouted. "I can't see him!"

The stampede rushed forward and all at once the herd plunged downwards.

"We're going down the riverbank!" Tess leaned back and gripped tightly as they approached the water.

Jamie gulped. "And we're not stopping!"

SPLASH!

Their Triceratops plunged into the churning river. The two friends were thrown into the water among the giant, thrashing dinosaurs and drowning insects.

Jamie swam up to the surface and held his hands out, keeping away from the dinosaurs' bodies and horns.

The huge dinosaurs stood in the water, seemingly relieved that the termites were being swept away by the river.

"They wanted to wash the termites off," Jamie managed to splutter.

"And us too!" Tess replied.

They felt the pull of the river and soon were sucked into the current.

"Thanks for the ride!" Jamie called out as they left their Triceratops taxi far behind.

Jamie heard a grunking noise nearby. "Wanna!" he cried. The little dinosaur was running along the riverbank trying to keep pace with them and he had something in his mouth.

"Your backpack!" Tess exclaimed. "It's safe!"

"Go Wanna!" shouted Jamie.

Jamie and Tess were both good swimmers, but the current was too strong to let them swim to the edge. When a log swept by, Jamie and Tess grabbed on to its stubby branches.

"Whew," gasped Tess as she got a good hold. She checked out the river ahead. "Do you think there are any Champsosauruses in here?"

"I hope not." Jamie groaned. "I think we've met enough prehistoric beasts for one day."

The log floated into a patch of shadow and Tess looked up. "It's Fang Rock!" she said. "We must be going towards Ginkgo Hill – and home!"

"Maybe it will take us all the way back, and save us the walk." Jamie grinned.

The river twisted around Fang Rock and out again into the sunshine. They could see Wanna on the bank. He was jumping up and down and grunking excitedly.

"What's the matter with Wanna?" Tess wondered aloud.

Jamie heard the sound of rushing water, and soon their log was being knocked this way and that between sharp rocks. The water churned and bubbled, and Jamie noticed that he could see the river ahead of them disappear. The land on either side of the river fell away and Jamie realized what Wanna was trying to warn them about. "It's a waterfall!"

Jamie and Tess kicked frantically towards the bank but the current was too strong. The log bumped and spun on towards the dangerous drop. Just before they were about to go over, the log caught suddenly between two rocks. They only just managed to hold on as white water crashed over their shoulders.

"Whew!" exclaimed Jamie. He could just see over the fall down to a large swirling pool below and was relieved that the log had saved them. He gave Tess a wobbly smile. "Let's get out of here."

creeeeak!

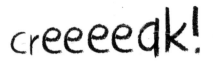

"What was that?" he gasped.

"The log's splitting from the force of the current!" yelled Tess. "We're going to go over the waterfall!"

Jamie caught at her arm. "Take a deep breath when you fall!" he shouted urgently. "Start swimming the moment you can!"

crack! The log broke and they were sucked through the white foaming water and over the edge.

CHAPTER 6

"Aaaah!" Jamie shouted as he plummeted down and down.

He took a huge breath just in time.

SPLASH!

He hit the churning water and plunged under the surface, tumbling around and around. Jamie felt the waterfall pushing him to the bottom of the river. He opened his eyes but it was dark and all he could see were bubbles swirling around him. He couldn't even tell which way up he was.

Then his foot touched rock. He pushed away hard, kicking his legs for all they were worth. At last he was at the surface, gulping in the wonderful air. He swam around, looking for Tess. He hoped his friend was alright!

Suddenly, the water beside him erupted and Tess bobbed up like a cork, gasping for breath.

Jamie and Tess looked up in awe at the huge waterfall they had just come over. "We made it!"

"A huge waterfall, an army of termites, a ride on a Triceratops," Tess said. "Another great adventure in Dino World!"

They swam away from the waterfall and let the gentle current take them downstream. Ahead there was a fork as the river split into two before it disappeared back into the jungle. The current swept them to the right where the trees were dense and tangled with creepers.

The river now became wider and slower. With weak strokes, they made their way to the side and grabbed hold of an overhanging branch.

"I can touch the bottom," gasped Tess. "There's a ledge."

They dragged themselves out of the water and collapsed on the safe, dry bank.

Grunk grunk!

Wanna bounded up and threw himself on them, head-butting and nudging at them in turn. Then he disappeared into the undergrowth and came back a moment later with the backpack in his mouth. He dropped it in front of them.

Jamie sat up. "He kept it safe! Well done, Wanna," he said, "you're a real friend. Now I can message Dinosaur Club later and tell them all about the Triceratops."

Tess reached over and got a ginkgo out of the bag. "You deserve this!" she said, giving it to Wanna. The little dinosaur gobbled it down.

"Yuck!" Tess cried, pushing him away. "Stink-o breath!"

"Where are we?" asked Jamie.

"Well you've got the map!" laughed Tess.

Jamie pulled it out and they had a look around. There was a steep slope ahead of them, covered in a thick wall of trees.

"I can just hear the waterfall," said Tess. She got to her feet and peered through the binoculars. "Yes, it's back there. It must be — look, there's the point of Fang Rock." She checked her compass. "It's east of here."

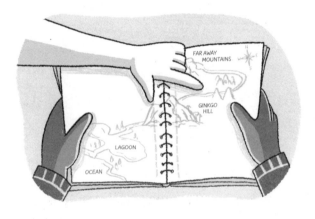

They looked at their map.

"And the river comes from the mountains in the north-east and flows across the plain." Jamie traced it with his finger.

"Then it goes through the jungle here – where we are," added Tess.

JUNGLE

Jamie gazed at the trees ahead of them. "Then we must be at the bottom of Ginkgo Hill. Told you it would save us the walk!"

Tess checked her watch. "Lucky this is waterproof." She grinned. "It's not long before the tide comes in. We don't want to get trapped on the cliffs."

Jamie nodded. "Granddad will be back from running the coastguard and he'll be wondering where we are." He picked up his backpack. "Who'd have thought making a map would be such an adventure?"

They climbed back up Ginkgo Hill. As they passed the break in the trees, Jamie looked back out over the plains. He could see the termite mounds in the distance, and beyond that, on the other side of the river, was the grazing Triceratops herd.

Wanna bounded along with them but as they reached the entrance to the cave, he slowed down and lowered his head.

Grunk?

"See you, Wanna," said Jamie, patting him on his hard, flat head. "We'll be back soon."

"And that's a promise!" added Tess. She pulled out the last two ginkgo fruit.

Wanna wagged his tail and gobbled up his treat happily.

Jamie and Tess stepped into the cave. Jamie placed his feet over the dinosaur footprints and felt the ground get harder as he went. On his fifth step, he was plunged into inky darkness, and he was back in the cave in Ammonite Bay. A moment later, Tess was standing next to him.

Jamie flicked on his torch and led the way out of the cave, down the rock fall,

and back along the path to the beach.

"What an adventure!" said Tess.

"Better than any theme park," agreed Jamie. He fished out his notebook and flicked to the map. "Look how far we travelled today! Right out onto the plain – and back the quick way!" He pointed to Fang Rock. "The waterfall was just here. What shall we call it?"

"Crashing Rock Falls!" declared Tess.

"Cool! I'll draw us going over the edge." Jamie grinned.

"Ahoy there, you two!" Granddad was in a rowing boat, guiding it towards the beach.

The friends waved and ran down to the sea.

"Come on," Granddad called. "I can't land the boat without your help."

Jamie and Tess jumped into the surf and waded out to the boat, helping Granddad pull the boat up the beach.

"When we're back home, Jamie," Granddad said, "you must show Tess the new Triceratops skull. It's sixty-six million years old." He grinned at Tess. "I bet you haven't seen anything like that before!"

Jamie and Tess smiled at each other too. Granddad would never believe what *they* had seen today in Dino World!

Dinosaur timeline

The Triassic
(250–200 million years ago)

The first period of the Mesozoic Era was the Triassic. During the Triassic, there were very few plants, and the Earth was hot and dry, like a desert. Most of the dinosaurs that lived during the Triassic were small.

The Jurassic
(200–145 million years ago)

The second period of the Mesozoic Era was the Jurassic. During the Jurassic, the Earth became cooler and wetter, which caused lots of plants to grow. This created lots of food for dinosaurs that helped them grow big and thrive.

The Cretaceous
(145–66 million years ago)

The third and final period of the Mesozoic Era was the Cretaceous. During the Cretaceous, dinosaurs were at their peak and dominated the Earth, but at the end, most of them suddenly became extinct.

Dinosaurs existed during a time on Earth known as the Mesozoic Era. It lasted for more than 180 million years, and was split into three different periods: the Triassic, Jurassic, and the Cretaceous.

Notable dinosaurs from the Triassic

Plateosaurus

Coelophysis

Eoraptor

Notable dinosaurs from the Jurassic

Stegosaurus

Allosaurus

Archaeopteryx

Diplodocus

Notable dinosaurs from the Cretaceous

T. rex

Triceratops

Velociraptor

Iguanodon

FAR AWAY MOUNTAINS

CRASHING
ROCK
FALLS

FANG
ROCK

GREAT PLAINS

GINKGO
HILL

DINO DATA

These plant-eating dinosaurs were about the size of an elephant. They were very strong, and their frills and horns helped protect them from predators.

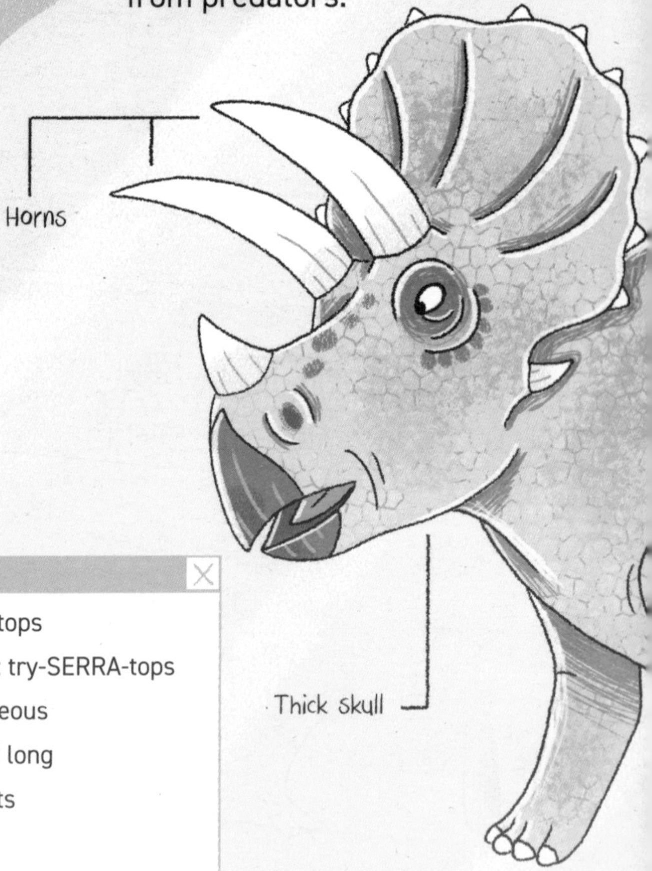

Horns

Thick skull

Name: Triceratops

Pronunciation: try-SERRA-tops

Period: Cretaceous

Size: 9m (30ft) long

Habitat: Forests

Diet: Plants

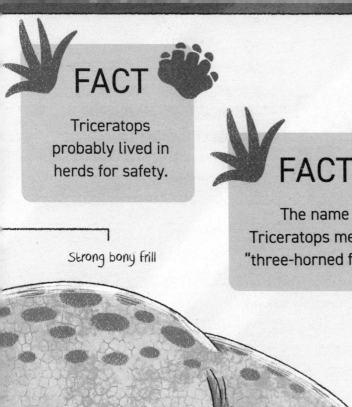

FACT

Triceratops probably lived in herds for safety.

FACT

The name Triceratops means "three-horned face".

Strong bony frill

DINO DATA

Alamosaurus was one of the biggest of the Cretaceous. It belonged to a group of huge dinosaurs called sauropods.

Name: Alamosaurus
Pronunciation: al-ah-muh-SORE-us
Period: Cretaceous
Size: 21m (68ft) long
Habitat: Plains and woodlands
Diet: Plants

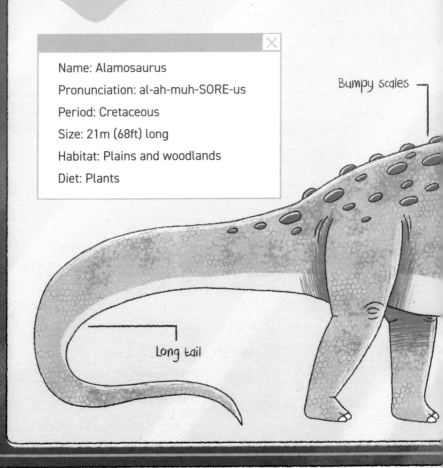

Bumpy scales

Long tail

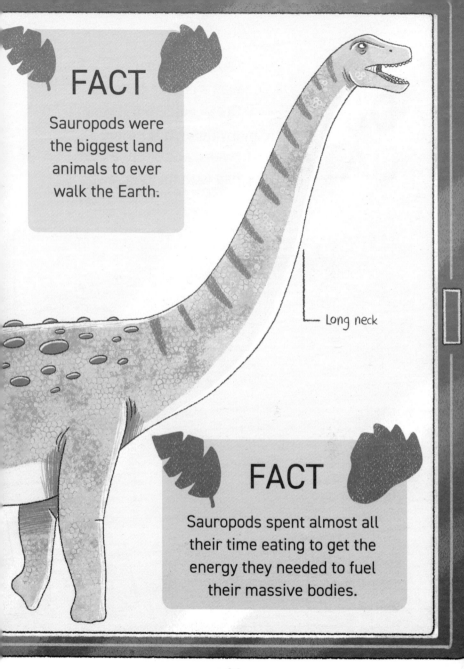

FACT

Sauropods were the biggest land animals to ever walk the Earth.

Long neck

FACT

Sauropods spent almost all their time eating to get the energy they needed to fuel their massive bodies.

DINO DATA

Champsosaurus was a reptile from the Cretaceous, but it wasn't a dinosaur. It lurked in rivers, and snapped up fish with its long jaws.

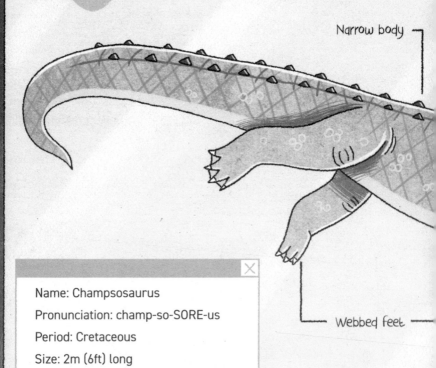

Narrow body

Webbed feet

Name: Champsosaurus

Pronunciation: champ-so-SORE-us

Period: Cretaceous

Size: 2m (6ft) long

Habitat: Rivers

Diet: Fish

FACT

Champsosaurus may look like a modern-day crocodile, but these animals aren't closely related at all.

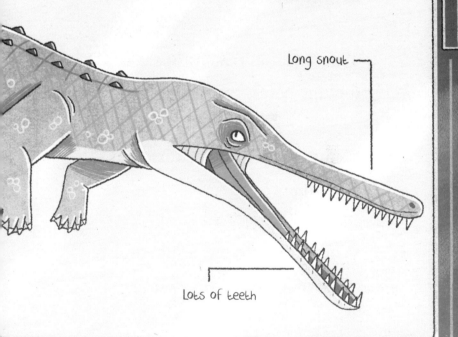

Long snout

Lots of teeth

QUIZ

1   True or false: Fossils are living things.

2   How many horns did Triceratops have?

3   True or false: Triceratops was a plant-eater.

4   What group of dinosaurs were the biggest?

5   What structure did Jamie and Tess mistake for houses?

6   True or false: Triceratops lived during the Jurassic period.

CHECK YOUR ANSWERS on page 95

GLOSSARY

AMMONITE
A type of sea creature that lived during the time of the dinosaurs

CARNIVORE
An animal that only eats meat

CRETACEOUS
The third period of the time dinosaurs existed (145-66 million years ago)

DINOSAUR
A group of ancient reptiles that lived millions of years ago

FOSSIL
Remains of a living thing that have become preserved over time

GINKGO
A type of tree that dates back
millions of years

HERBIVORE
An animal that only eats plant matter

PALAEONTOLOGIST
A scientist who studies dinosaurs
and other fossils

PTEROSAUR
Ancient flying reptiles that existed at
the same time as dinosaurs

PREDATOR
An animal that hunts other
animals for food

QUIZ ANSWERS
1. False
2. Three
3. True
4. Sauropods
5. Termite nests
6. False

Text for DK by Working Partners Ltd
9 Kingsway, London WC2B 6XF
With special thanks to Jan Burchett and Sara Vogler

Design by Collaborate Ltd
Illustrator Louise Forshaw
Consultant Emily Keeble

Acquisitions Editor James Mitchem
Senior Designer and Jacket Designer Elle Ward
Publishing Coordinator Issy Walsh
Production Editor Abi Maxwell
Production Controller Isabell Schart
Publishing Director Sarah Larter

First published in Great Britain in 2022 by
Dorling Kindersley Limited
One Embassy Gardens, 8 Viaduct Gardens,
London, SW11 7AY

A CIP catalogue record for this book
is available from the British Library.
ISBN: 978-0-2415-3341-3

Printed and bound in Great Britain by
Clays Ltd, Elcograf S.p.A.

www.dk.com
For the curious

The publisher would like to thank Jo Chukualim and Lynne Murray for
picture library assistance, and Caroline Twomey for proofreading.

This book was made with Forest Stewardship Council ™
certified paper – one small step in DK's commitment
to a sustainable future. For more information go to
www.dk.com/our-green-pledge